MY SISTER CELIA

by JUDITH CASELEY

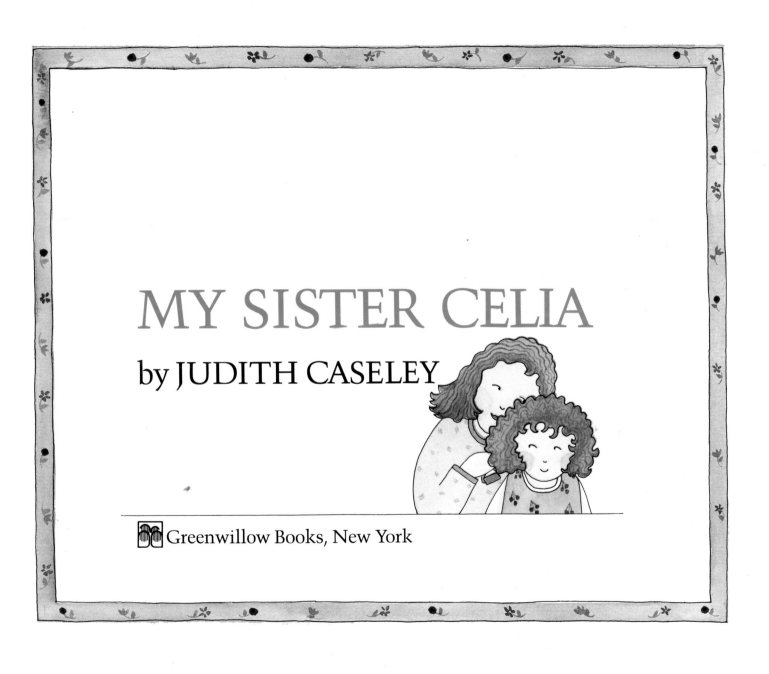

Greenwillow Books, New York

Library of Congress Cataloging-in-Publication Data

Caseley, Judith.   My sister Celia.
Summary: When her sister Celia prepares for her wedding,
Emma misses the quiet, private times they used to share.
[1. Sisters—Fiction] I. Title.   PZ7.C2677My 1986
[E]   85-27211   ISBN 0-688-06483-3
ISBN 0-688-06484-1 (lib. bdg.)

Watercolor paints and colored pencils were combined with a separate black-ink line for the full-color art.
The typeface is Trump Medieval.

TO BARA, JEANNIE,
AND LARRY,
WITH LOVE

"My sister, Celia, is the best sister in the whole wide world,"
Emma always said to her best friend, ~~Debbie.~~ DECCA

Celia was a lot older than
Emma. She had an apartment
of her own. But every weekend
she saved a day just for Emma.
They drank coffee together, but Emma's was fake. Celia
made hot chocolate milk and poured it into a coffee cup.
Sometimes she curled Emma's hair. When she took out
the rollers, she laughed and called Emma "my sister the
poodle."

They drew pictures together. They made one of Mama and Papa. Celia laughed when she drew Papa's bald head. Emma drew a hat right on top.

"Papa doesn't like being bald," she said.

They took walks together. One day it rained, and Emma got her foot stuck in the mud. When she pulled it out, her boot was gone. Celia reached into the mud puddle and found Emma's boot. When they got home they were so muddy that their mother called them "the home wreckers."

Sometimes they went to the movies. Celia liked the old ones. They ate popcorn, and Celia cried when the boy had to leave the girl.

Every year they watched *The Wizard of Oz* on television. Mama said it was a tradition. Emma's favorite part was when Dorothy clicked her red ruby shoes together and said, "There's no place like home."

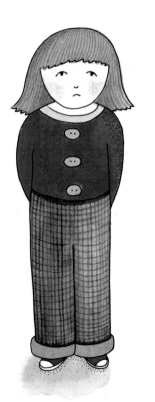

One week, on Emma's special day,
Celia brought home a friend named
Ben. That day Celia didn't curl
Emma's hair or make fake coffee or
bake brownies or take Emma on a hike.
She talked to Mama and Papa and
hardly talked to Emma at all.

The next week was just the same. Emma drew
a picture of Celia and ~~Ben~~ DOUG, and Celia just
said, "Emma, you made ~~Ben~~ DOUG much too small."
"So what," said Emma.

"I don't like ~~Ben~~ Doug," Emma told ~~Debbie~~ DECCA. "I miss
my special day."
~~Debbie~~ DECCA said, "I think Celia is getting married."
"She is not!" shouted Emma.
Then Emma found a magazine on the couch
called *You're a Bride.*
"It isn't true," she said to ~~Debbie~~ DECCA, "because
Celia would have told me."

The next weekend Celia showed Emma a ring on
her left hand and said, "~~Ben~~ Doug and I are engaged."
The ring was a ruby, and it was red, like Dorothy's
shoes in *The Wizard of Oz.*
"Do you like it?" asked Celia.
"No," said Emma.

"You'll be my flower girl," said Celia.
"No, I won't," said Emma.

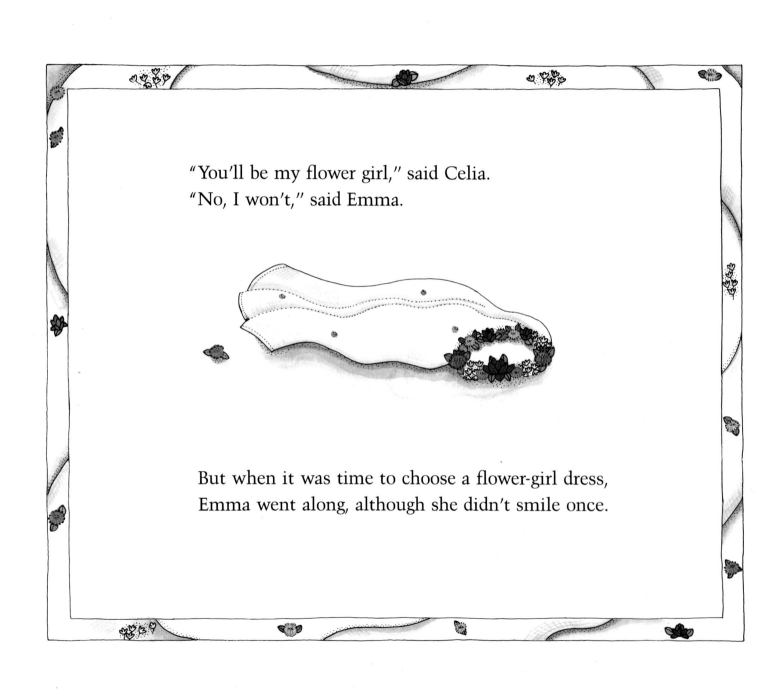

But when it was time to choose a flower-girl dress,
Emma went along, although she didn't smile once.

The next week Emma went to the florist
to help choose the wedding flowers.
"I like this big red one," she said.
"An amaryllis is not right for a wedding,"
Mama said.

When they got home, Emma ran to the basement
and sat in the dark.
"Emma!" called Celia. "Where are you?"
Emma didn't answer.
Celia came downstairs.
"We'll have our special day again soon," she said.
Emma didn't say a word.
"Come up and have some coffee," said Celia, "and
then I have to go."
"No," said Emma.

Later, when Emma went upstairs, there was a cup
of fake coffee and a big box on the table.
The note on the box said, "Emma—To be worn at
my wedding. Love, Celia."
Emma smiled, just a little, and drank her coffee.

The day of the wedding Mama yelled at Papa for
washing the dog.
"It calms me down," said Papa.
They all got ready and drove downtown.
Before the ceremony they had their pictures taken.
Soon the guests arrived.

At last the music began. The bridesmaids walked
down the aisle. Then it was Emma's turn.
Down the aisle she came, wearing her brand-new
Wizard of Oz ruby-red shoes.
Then came Celia, looking like a princess.
As she passed Emma, she winked.

The next year Emma watched *The Wizard of Oz*
with Celia and ~~Ben~~ Doug and her new nephew, ~~Evan~~. Fido
"It's a tradition," she told ~~Evan~~. Fido
But ~~Evan~~ was too young to understand.
Fido